A Healing from Heaven

Spines

A Healing from Heaven

KAREN LEWIS

DEDICATION

This book is dedicated to my family for their unwavering support.

And to Pastor Donald Mapes, whose guidance and presence have profoundly shaped my life.

Acknowledgments

I would like to express my heartfelt gratitude to the following individuals for their support and inspiration throughout the creation of this book:

- **My family**, for their unwavering love and constant encouragement.

- **My friends**, for their steadfast belief in my writing and ongoing support.

- **My editor, [Wardah]**, for their invaluable feedback and insightful guidance.

- **The readers**, for your interest and enthusiasm, which fuel my passion for storytelling.

Thank you all for being an integral part of this journey.

Heavenly Father,

We come before You with grateful hearts, seeking Your presence and guidance as we embark on this journey of faith through the words written in these pages. We ask for Your Holy Spirit to fill us with wisdom and understanding, that we may be drawn closer to You and grow in our knowledge of Your love and grace.

Lord, we dedicate this book to Your glory. May it be a source of inspiration, comfort, and encouragement to all who read it. Let every word be an instrument of Your peace, hope, and truth. We pray that through these reflections, stories, and teachings, many will find strength in their trials, joy in their blessings, and a deeper relationship with You.

Bless the readers with open hearts and minds, ready to receive Your message. Guide them in their spiritual journey, and may Your light shine brightly upon their paths. We trust in Your divine plan and ask that Your will be done in our lives.

In Jesus' name, we pray.

CONTENTS

CHAPTER 1

HEAVEN

Heaven, a place of pure bliss and joy, invites every soul with an embrace of unending love and peace. The air here is filled with the sweet scent of flowers, a fragrance so delicate and pure that it feels like a gentle kiss on the senses. As you take in a breath, the harmonious voices of angels singing in perfect unity fill your ears, creating a symphony that resonates with the very essence of your being.

Walking along the streets, you notice they are paved with gold, each step reflecting the eternal light that illuminates this divine realm. The gold is not like any earthly metal; it shimmers with a brilliance that speaks of eternity and purity, a reminder of the everlasting promise made to those who believe. The buildings, towering majestically, are crafted from shimmering crystal, their surfaces catching the light and scattering it in a dazzling array of colors.

In heaven, every corner reveals a new wonder, each more breathtaking than the last. The landscape is adorned with lush gardens, where flowers of every hue bloom in perfect harmony. These gardens are not mere patches of beauty but living testimonies to the Creator's boundless creativity and love. Streams of crystal-clear water flow gently through the gardens, their soothing sounds adding to the serene ambiance.

As you move deeper into this celestial paradise, the feeling of joy becomes overwhelming. There is no sorrow, no pain, no suffering—only a profound sense of well-being and contentment. This is a place where the soul finds its true home, a sanctuary where love and healing abound. Here, in the presence of the Divine, every wound is healed, every heartache soothed, and every tear wiped away.

Heaven is more than a destination; it is the fulfillment of every promise, the culmination of every hope, and the realization of every dream. It is a place where the weary find rest, the broken find healing, and the lost find their way. In this sacred space, the soul is renewed, and the spirit is uplifted, bathed in the light of God's unending love and grace.

The air in heaven is imbued with the sweet fragrance of flowers, a scent so delicate and pure that it feels like a gentle caress on the senses. As you breathe it in, the harmonious voices of angels singing in perfect unity fill your ears, creating a symphony that resonates deep within your soul.

Strolling along the streets, you notice they are paved with gold, each step reflecting the eternal light that bathes this divine realm. Unlike any earthly metal, this gold glows with a brilliance that symbolizes eternity and purity, a testament to the everlasting promise made to the faithful. The buildings, standing majestically, are constructed from shimmering crystal, their surfaces catching and scattering the light in a dazzling array of colors.

Every corner of heaven reveals a new marvel, each more breathtaking than the last. The landscape is adorned with lush gardens where flowers of every color bloom in perfect harmony. These gardens are not just patches of beauty but living testaments to the Creator's boundless creativity and love. Crystal-clear streams flow gently through the gardens, their soothing sounds enhancing the serene ambiance.

At the heart of this divine splendor lies the true essence of heaven: its inhabitants. Filled with love and peace, every soul here radiates a joy that reflects the pure bliss of being in the presence of the Divine. There is no pain, no suffering, no sorrow—only an overwhelming sense of well-being and contentment. The colors around you are more vibrant than any seen on earth, each hue more vivid and alive, as if painted by the hand of God Himself.

The music in heaven is more melodic, each note a perfect blend of harmony and grace. It fills the air with tranquility and joy, a constant reminder of the eternal celebration that takes place in this holy realm. The laughter of the inhabitants is infectious, a joyous sound that echoes through the streets and gardens, uplifting the spirits of all who hear it. This laughter is not just an expression of happiness but a testament to the complete absence of fear, worry, and sadness.

As we explore this heavenly realm, we are enveloped by a sense of wonder and awe that fills every moment with divine splendor. The beauty of the gardens is unlike anything seen on earth. Lush, verdant landscapes stretch as far as the eye can see, filled with flowers of every imaginable color and variety. Each bloom seems to radiate a light of its own, their petals shimmering in the celestial glow. Trees laden with fruit that glisten like jewels offer their bounty freely, their fragrance mingling with the sweet scent of blossoms to create an intoxicating aroma. Birds with feathers of iridescent hues flit among the branches, their songs adding to the symphony of nature that fills the air.

Venturing further, we come upon the majesty of the throne room, a place of unparalleled grandeur and reverence. The throne itself, a symbol of ultimate authority and grace, is made of the finest gold and encrusted with precious stones that sparkle with a divine light. Surrounding the throne are countless angels, their wings a dazzling array of white and gold, singing praises in perfect harmony. The atmosphere is charged with a palpable sense of holiness, a sacred energy that fills every heart with awe and humility.

In this heavenly realm, we witness the joy of reunions between loved ones, a sight that brings tears of happiness to the eyes. Families and friends, separated by the bounds of earthly life, are reunited in embraces that convey a love unbroken by time or distance. The joy in these moments is pure and overwhelming, a testament to the enduring power of love that transcends all earthly boundaries. Laughter and tears of joy mingle as stories are shared and bonds are rekindled, each reunion a celebration of love's triumph over death.

Amidst these scenes of beauty and joy, we also witness the celebration of victories won. Saints and heroes of faith are honored for their perseverance and faithfulness, their lives a testament to the power of divine grace. Their stories are shared and celebrated, not as mere tales of past struggles but as living testimonies of victory and redemption.

Crowns of glory are placed upon their heads, and their names are inscribed in the Book of Life, their deeds remembered and cherished for all eternity.

Everywhere we look, heaven reveals its wonders, each sight a glimpse into the infinite beauty and majesty of the Divine. The sense of wonder and awe that fills our hearts is a constant reminder of the boundless love and grace that permeates this heavenly realm, a foretaste of the eternal joy that awaits all who enter its gates.

The happiness that permeates heaven is pure and unending. It is not dependent on circumstances or fleeting pleasures but rooted in the eternal joy of being in the presence of the Almighty. Every moment is filled with a deep and abiding gladness, a joy that springs from the very essence of our souls. This happiness is contagious, spreading from one soul to another, creating a symphony of joy that echoes through the halls of heaven.

Heaven is also a place of rest and rejuvenation. After the trials and tribulations of earthly life, it offers a sanctuary where we can lay down our burdens and find true rest. Our souls, weary from the journey, are refreshed and renewed in this divine refuge. Here, we find the strength we need to continue, the peace that fills our hearts, and the rejuvenation that restores our spirits. It is a place where we can breathe deeply and fully, free from the constraints and pressures of the world.

In this heavenly realm, our souls find true fulfillment and contentment. Every longing, every desire, every need is met in the presence of the Divine. We are no longer searching, no longer striving, but finally at home in the embrace of God's love. This fulfillment is complete and total, filling every part of our being with a deep and abiding contentment. It is the fulfillment of every promise, the realization of every hope, and the completion of every journey.

Here, we are free to be our true selves, unburdened by the masks and facades we wore in earthly life. In the light of God's love, we can finally be who we were always meant to be, our true and authentic selves. This freedom is liberating and exhilarating, allowing us to explore the depths of our souls and the heights of our potential. We are no longer bound by fear or doubt but free to live fully and completely in the light of God's love.

Basking in the glory of God's love forevermore, we find our ultimate purpose and meaning. This love is the source of all joy, peace, and fulfillment, an unending wellspring that nourishes our souls and fills our hearts. In this divine embrace, we are cherished and valued, known and loved, celebrated and honored. It is a love that never fades, never diminishes, but grows stronger and deeper with each passing moment.

This eternal peace and happiness, this rest and rejuvenation, this fulfillment and freedom, this basking in the glory of God's love—this is the promise of heaven, the ultimate destination for our souls. It is a place where every tear is wiped away, every sorrow is turned to joy, and every heart is made whole. It is the fulfillment of God's promise, the realization of His love, and the culmination of His grace. Here, in this heavenly realm, we find our true home, our eternal rest, and our everlasting joy.

CHAPTER 2
RELATIONSHIP WITH GOD

Having a relationship with God is a deeply personal and spiritual journey that can bring immense joy, peace, and fulfillment to one's life. It involves developing a sense of connection, trust, and communication with a higher power that is believed to be loving, compassionate, and all-knowing.

Embarking on this journey requires an openness of heart and mind, a willingness to explore and embrace the divine presence in every aspect of our lives. It begins with a desire to know God, to understand His nature, and to experience His love firsthand. This desire leads us to seek Him through prayer, meditation, and the study of sacred texts. These practices become the foundation of our relationship with God, creating a space where we can encounter His presence and hear His voice.

Developing a connection with God is not a one-time event but a continuous process of growth and deepening intimacy. It is nurtured through daily interactions, moments of quiet reflection, and the practice of gratitude. In these moments, we open our hearts to God's love, allowing it to fill us and transform us. We begin to see His hand in the beauty of creation, in the kindness of others, and in the quiet whispers of our souls. This connection brings a profound sense of belonging and purpose, reminding us that we are never alone and that we are deeply loved.

Trust is a cornerstone of our relationship with God. It involves surrendering our fears, doubts, and anxieties, placing them in His capable hands. Trusting God means believing that He is always with us, guiding us, and working for our good, even when we cannot see the path ahead. It is the assurance that His plans for us are filled with hope and promise, that He knows us better than we know ourselves, and that His love for us is unwavering. This trust brings peace to our hearts, allowing us to navigate life's challenges with confidence and serenity.

Communication with God is the lifeblood of our relationship. It is through prayer that we speak to Him, sharing our joys, our sorrows, our hopes, and our fears. Prayer is not just about asking for things but about building a relationship, listening for His guidance, and expressing our love and gratitude. It is a dialogue that deepens our connection and helps us align our hearts with His will. In moments of silence and stillness, we can hear His gentle whispers, offering comfort, wisdom, and direction.

Understanding God's nature as loving, compassionate, and all-knowing transforms the way we relate to Him. We come to see Him not as a distant, impersonal force but as a caring Father, a faithful Friend, and a wise Counselor. His compassion reassures us that He cares about every detail of our lives, that He is moved by our struggles, and that He is always ready to extend His mercy and grace. His all-knowing nature gives us confidence that nothing escapes His notice, that He understands our deepest needs and desires, and that He is always working to bring about the best for us.

For many people, having a relationship with God involves prayer, meditation, and reflection on spiritual teachings. It can also involve participating in religious rituals, attending worship services, and seeking guidance from spiritual leaders or mentors.

Prayer is a fundamental practice in cultivating a relationship with God. It is a conversation with the Divine, a moment to express gratitude, seek guidance, and share our deepest hopes and fears. Through prayer, we open our hearts to God's presence, inviting His wisdom and comfort into our lives. Whether spoken aloud or in silent contemplation, prayer strengthens our connection with God and aligns our hearts with His will.

Meditation provides a quiet space for listening to God's voice and discerning His guidance. It involves stilling our minds and hearts, allowing us to become receptive to spiritual insights and divine inspiration. In meditation, we reflect on sacred truths and seek to deepen our understanding of God's love and purpose for our lives. It is a practice that fosters inner peace and spiritual growth, helping us to live more consciously and aligned with God's intentions.

Reflection on spiritual teachings enriches our understanding of God's character and His plan for humanity. Studying scriptures and spiritual texts allows us to delve deeper into the timeless wisdom and truths that offer guidance and comfort. Through reflection, we gain insight into God's promises, His faithfulness throughout history, and His enduring love for His creation. This deepens our faith and nurtures a profound sense of trust in His divine providence.

Participating in religious rituals serves as a tangible expression of our devotion and reverence for God. Rituals such as sacraments, ceremonies, and observances are sacred acts that connect us to the traditions and beliefs of our faith community. They serve to commemorate significant events, express gratitude, seek forgiveness, and renew our spiritual commitment. Engaging in these rituals fosters a sense of belonging and unity within the community of believers, reinforcing our shared faith and values.

Attending worship services is a communal practice that allows us to join with others in praising and worshiping God. It is a time of collective prayer, singing hymns of praise, and listening to teachings that inspire and uplift our spirits. Worship services provide a sacred space where we can draw near to God, experience His presence among fellow believers, and receive spiritual nourishment through shared fellowship and worship.

Seeking guidance from spiritual leaders or mentors provides invaluable support and counsel on our spiritual journey. These individuals, often seasoned in faith and wisdom, offer guidance, encouragement, and prayerful support as we navigate life's challenges and seek to grow in our relationship with God. They provide insights drawn from their own experiences and understanding of spiritual principles, helping us to deepen our faith, overcome obstacles, and stay grounded in God's truth.

Having a relationship with God can also inspire feelings of gratitude, humility, and awe at the beauty and wonder of the world around us.

When facing challenges, the assurance of God's presence brings a deep sense of comfort. Knowing that we are not alone but held in the embrace of His love gives us the courage to endure hardship with resilience and faith. Through prayer and meditation, we find solace in His promises, finding peace in the midst of turmoil and strength in times of weakness. This divine comfort is a source of unwavering support, guiding us through life's storms and reassuring us of His steadfast presence.

A relationship with God provides a profound sense of purpose and direction in life. By seeking His will and aligning our actions with His divine plan, we discover clarity and meaning in our journey. God's guidance illuminates our path, helping us make decisions that honor Him and serve others. This sense of purpose instills a deep fulfillment, knowing that our lives are part of a greater, eternal purpose ordained by a loving Creator.

God's presence inspires a heart overflowing with gratitude for His blessings and provision. We are humbled by His grace and mercy, recognizing our dependence on Him for every good gift. This humility cultivates a reverence for His majesty and a profound awe at the beauty and wonder of His creation. From the intricate details of nature to the depths of human experience, every moment becomes an opportunity to marvel at His handiwork and acknowledge His sovereignty.

It is a journey of faith and spiritual growth that can lead to a deeper understanding of oneself and one's place in the universe. Each person's relationship with God is unique, shaped by personal encounters, spiritual insights, and moments of divine presence. It is a journey where faith intertwines with life experiences, shaping beliefs and perspectives. Through prayer and contemplation, individuals forge a connection with the divine that resonates with their deepest aspirations and desires. This personal relationship provides a sanctuary of solace and spiritual renewal, where hearts find rest and souls find nourishment.

The presence of God infuses life with a profound sense of peace that transcends circumstances. In moments of prayer and meditation, His peace washes over troubled hearts, offering reassurance and calm. This inner peace coexists with a joy that springs from knowing God's love and experiencing His grace. It is a joy that surpasses fleeting happiness rooted in the eternal promises of faith. Through this relationship, individuals discover a fulfillment that satisfies the deepest longings of the soul, finding purpose in serving God and others with love and compassion.

Embracing a relationship with God is a journey marked by spiritual growth and transformation. It involves seeking His presence in daily life, learning from His teachings, and embodying His values of love, forgiveness, and compassion. This journey deepens faith as individuals wrestle with questions, seek understanding, and cultivate a deeper intimacy with the divine. It is a continuous process of seeking truth, embracing challenges, and experiencing divine revelations that shape character and enrich spiritual maturity.

Through the lens of faith, individuals gain insights into their identity, purpose, and role in the universe. They discover their inherent worth as beloved children of God, embraced by His unconditional love. This understanding fosters a sense of interconnectedness with all creation, recognizing the divine presence in every aspect of life. It empowers individuals to live authentically, guided by spiritual principles that honor God and reflect His goodness in relationships, work, and community.

CHAPTER 3
PRAYER

There are many verses throughout the Bible that talk about the importance and power of prayer. One of the most profound passages on this topic is found in Philippians 4:6-7 . This passage advises us not to be anxious about anything but to bring every concern to God through prayer and petition with thanksgiving. It promises that the peace of God, which transcends all understanding, will guard our hearts and minds in Christ Jesus.

Prayer is a cornerstone of the Christian faith, offering a direct line of communication with God. It is through prayer that we express our deepest thoughts, concerns, and desires to the Divine. The Bible emphasizes that prayer is not just a ritualistic practice but a vital aspect of our relationship with God. It is an avenue for seeking guidance, asking for strength, and offering gratitude. The act of praying invites God's presence into our lives, providing a means for us to connect with His wisdom and grace.

Philippians 4:6-7 offers a powerful antidote to anxiety. In moments of worry and distress, the passage encourages us to turn to God with our prayers and petitions. By doing so, we relinquish our anxieties and trust that God is in control. This practice of bringing our concerns before God with a spirit of thanksgiving shifts our focus from our problems to His promises. It transforms our approach to challenges, allowing us to experience a sense of peace that transcends our understanding—a peace that comes from knowing that God is working on our behalf and that we are not alone in our struggles.

The peace promised in Philippians 4:6-7 is not merely the absence of conflict but a profound inner tranquility that comes from a deep trust in God's sovereignty. This peace guards our hearts and minds, protecting us from the turmoil and uncertainty that often accompany life's difficulties. It acts as a shield, calming our fears and restoring our sense of security. This divine peace is a tangible manifestation of God's presence in our lives, reassuring us that He is with us in every moment and that His love and care are unwavering.

Prayer holds transformative power. It is through prayer that we align our will with God's, seeking His guidance and intervention in our lives. The act of praying not only invites God's presence but also opens our hearts to receive His blessings and wisdom. Through prayer, we can experience personal growth, healing, and renewal. It strengthens our faith, builds our character, and deepens our relationship with God. As we pray, we become more attuned to His voice, more receptive to His direction, and more aware of His hand at work in our lives.

Developing a robust prayer life involves making prayer a regular part of our daily routine. It requires intentionality and commitment, setting aside time to engage in conversation with God. This can be through structured prayers, spontaneous expressions of gratitude, or contemplative moments of silence. As we cultivate our prayer life, we discover new dimensions of our relationship with God, experiencing His presence in profound and personal ways.

Another important verse is **Matthew 6:6**, which provides profound guidance on the nature of our prayer life. This verse instructs us to pray in private, emphasizing the deeply personal and intimate nature of our communication with God. It tells us to go into our room, close the door, and pray to our Father who is unseen. The verse assures us that our Father, who sees what is done in secret, will reward us. This highlights the sincerity and humility that should accompany our prayers.

Matthew 6:6 underscores that prayer is fundamentally a private and personal experience between the individual and God. It invites us to retreat from the public eye and enter into a space of solitude where our communication with God can be sincere and unencumbered by external influences. This private setting allows us to express our thoughts, desires, and needs with authenticity, free from the need for validation or approval from others. It is in this intimate space that we can engage in a genuine dialogue with God, sharing our deepest concerns and joys.

The instruction to go into our room and close the door symbolizes the importance of creating a sacred space for prayer. It suggests setting aside time and space that is dedicated solely to our relationship with God. This act of retreating into privacy helps to eliminate distractions and create an environment where we can focus entirely on our conversation with God. It reflects a commitment to prioritizing our spiritual connection and making room for a meaningful encounter with the Divine.

The verse emphasizes that we pray to our Father who is unseen, reminding us of the nature of God as a spiritual being who transcends the physical realm. This unseen aspect of God invites us to trust in His presence and faithfulness, even though we cannot see Him with our physical eyes. It encourages us to cultivate faith and confidence in God's ability to hear and respond to our prayers, regardless of our limited human perspective.

Matthew 6:6 highlights the importance of approaching prayer with sincerity and humility. The act of praying in secret reflects a heart that seeks to communicate with God out of genuine desire rather than for the sake of public recognition. It underscores the idea that our prayers should be driven by a heartfelt connection with God, rather than by a desire for external validation or accolades. This sincerity and humility in prayer align with the biblical principle that God values the intentions of our hearts more than outward appearances.

The verse assures us that our Father, who sees what is done in secret, will reward us. This promise of reward is not necessarily a material blessing but a deeper spiritual fulfillment and intimacy with God. The reward comes in the form of spiritual growth, increased understanding, and a strengthened relationship with the Divine. It signifies that our sincere and private prayers are valued and honored by God, leading to a richer and more rewarding spiritual experience.

1 Thessalonians 5:16-18 provides a powerful framework for our approach to prayer and spirituality. This passage encourages us to rejoice always, pray continually, and give thanks in all circumstances. It describes this continuous and thankful approach to prayer as God's will for us in Christ Jesus. This underscores the importance of maintaining a joyful and grateful spirit in our prayer life, regardless of our circumstances.

The command to "rejoice always" reflects an invitation to cultivate a spirit of joy that transcends our immediate circumstances. Rejoicing is not merely an emotional response to favorable conditions but a deliberate choice to celebrate God's goodness and faithfulness in every aspect of life. This joy stems from recognizing God's presence and promises, even in the midst of trials and difficulties. It is an expression of deep trust in His sovereignty and an acknowledgment of the countless blessings He bestows upon us. By choosing to rejoice always, we align our hearts with the divine perspective, finding reasons for gratitude and celebration even when faced with challenges.

The exhortation to "pray continually" emphasizes the importance of maintaining a consistent and ongoing dialogue with God. This does not imply that we must be in a constant state of formal prayer but encourages a mindset of constant connection with the Divine. It invites us to integrate prayer into the rhythm of our daily lives, turning to God in moments of joy, sorrow, decision-making, and everyday activities. Continual prayer fosters a deeper relationship with God, making Him a central part of our lives and enabling us to seek His guidance and comfort throughout each day.

The instruction to "give thanks in all circumstances" underscores the significance of gratitude in our spiritual practice. Regardless of our situation—whether we are experiencing abundance or facing adversity—thanksgiving is a vital aspect of our relationship with God. This gratitude is rooted in the understanding that God is always at work, guiding, providing, and sustaining us. By expressing thanks in every circumstance, we acknowledge God's hand in our lives and affirm our trust in His goodness and providence. This attitude of gratitude transforms our perspective, helping us to focus on God's faithfulness rather than our difficulties.

The passage describes this continuous and thankful approach to prayer as God's will for us in Christ Jesus. This declaration highlights that rejoicing, continual prayer, and thanksgiving are not merely recommended practices but are aligned with God's desires for His people. Embracing these practices reflects our commitment to living out our faith in a way that honors God and demonstrates our trust in His plan. It affirms that our spiritual well-being and growth are intricately linked to maintaining a joyful and grateful attitude in all aspects of life.

Incorporating these principles into our daily lives has profound effects on our spiritual well-being. A joyful, prayerful, and thankful heart fosters a deeper sense of peace and contentment, regardless of external circumstances. It helps us to remain resilient in the face of adversity and to recognize and appreciate the blessings that we might otherwise overlook. This approach to prayer and spirituality not only strengthens our relationship with God but also enhances our overall outlook on life, making us more attuned to His presence and purpose in our lives.

James 5:16 provides profound insights into the communal aspect of prayer and its role in bringing about healing and righteousness. The verse advises us to confess our sins to one another and pray for each other, emphasizing that this practice is integral to experiencing healing. It underscores that the prayer of a righteous person is both powerful and effective, reflecting the significant impact that sincere and righteous prayers can have on our lives and the lives of others.

The act of confessing our sins to one another is not merely about admitting our wrongdoings but about fostering transparency and accountability within our community. By sharing our struggles and seeking support, we create a space for mutual encouragement and healing. This confession is a step towards personal and collective growth, allowing us to acknowledge our faults and seek forgiveness, which in turn opens the door for God's grace and restoration.

Praying for each other further amplifies the communal nature of this practice. When we lift one another up in prayer, we engage in a shared spiritual journey, interceding on behalf of others and seeking God's intervention in their lives. This collective act of prayer fosters a sense of unity and solidarity within the community. It reinforces the idea that we are not alone in our struggles but are supported by a network of faith that holds us up in times of need.

The verse highlights that the prayer of a righteous person is especially powerful and effective. This underscores the importance of living a life aligned with God's will and embodying righteousness. Such prayers, offered with sincere hearts and pure intentions, carry a weight of spiritual authority and can effect real change. The effectiveness of these prayers is a testament to the divine partnership between our earnest requests and God's ability to bring about transformation.

By emphasizing the communal and powerful nature of prayer, James 5:16 teaches us that healing and righteousness are not achieved in isolation but through a network of supportive, prayerful relationships. It invites us to engage actively in the spiritual well-being of others, recognizing that our prayers and confessions contribute to a larger tapestry of divine work. This interconnectedness in prayer fosters a deeper sense of community, where individuals are both contributors to and recipients of God's healing grace.

Ultimately, the verse reinforces that prayer is a dynamic and communal practice, where the collective faith and righteousness of the community play a crucial role in bringing about spiritual and physical healing. It challenges us to embrace a more profound and active role in each other's spiritual lives, understanding that our prayers have the power to effect meaningful change and foster a healing environment within our communities.

In moments of uncertainty or difficulty, prayer provides a pathway to find peace. It offers a space to release our anxieties and burdens, trusting that God is attentive to our needs and capable of providing comfort and assurance. Through prayer, we invite God's presence into our lives, allowing His peace to transcend our understanding and guard our hearts and minds. This peace is not merely the absence of conflict but a profound sense of serenity that comes from knowing that we are held and cared for by a loving and all-powerful God.

Moreover, prayer is a powerful tool for experiencing the transformative power of God's presence. When we pray, we open ourselves to the movement of the Holy Spirit, inviting God's love and grace to manifest in our lives. This connection fosters a sense of intimacy with God, making His presence more tangible and real. The act of praying brings us into direct contact with the divine, allowing us to experience His transformative power, healing, and guidance in a personal and meaningful way.

The verses also highlight that prayer is not just a routine practice but a dynamic and powerful experience. It enables us to encounter God's love and grace in our daily lives, enriching our spiritual journey. Through prayer, we can sense His active involvement in our lives, receive His strength and encouragement, and feel His unconditional love. This connection through prayer nurtures our faith, builds our spiritual resilience, and deepens our understanding of God's character and His plans for us.

CHAPTER 4

GRACE

The grace of God stands as one of the deepest and most transforming ideas within the Christian faith, permeating the entirety of its theology and practice. Fundamentally, grace is the valuable and undeserved favor that God has shown to humans; it is a manifestation of His limitless mercy, love, and compassion. It is given to everyone as a divine gift, reflecting God's fundamental character as an infinitely good entity, and is neither earned nor deserved by human effort or righteousness. It is the foundation on which the majestic faith stands.

According to Christian doctrine, grace is an active and dynamic energy that molds the relationship between the Creator and His creation, not just a kind disposition or passive kindness from God. Theologians refer to grace as the fundamental cornerstone around which the entire structure of salvation and redemption is constructed. Fallen humanity, tarnished by sin and cut off from God, is offered forgiveness, reconciliation, and eventually eternal life via grace.

One of the most fundamental tenets of Christian theology is the interweaving of the concepts of original sin and grace, which highlights the extreme severity of human separation from God and the boundless extent of God's mercy. According to the theory of original sin, which is presented in the first few chapters of Genesis, humanity descended from a state of original righteousness into spiritual corruption and death as a result of Adam and Eve's transgression in the Garden of Eden. Sin was brought into the human condition by this "fall," not only as a personal shortcoming but also as an inherited condition that impacts everyone on the planet. "Therefore, just as sin entered the world through one man, and death through sin, and in this way death came to all people, because all sinned," the apostle Paul states in **Romans 5:12.**

The idea of original sin addresses the deep estrangement and brokenness that exist in the connection between God and humans. Humanity is spiritually dead in its fallen state and unable to achieve righteousness or contact with God on its own. **Isaiah 64:6** stresses this fact with startling clarity: "All of us have become like one who is unclean, and all our righteous acts are like filthy rags." This demonstrates the pointlessness of human endeavors to attain purity or merit in the sight of an all-powerful and holy God.

This is further explained in the work Confessions by the early Church founder Augustine of Hippo (354–430 AD), a pivotal figure in the formation of Western Christian thought: "The chains of my sinfulness bound me, yet I was unwilling to be free." I was a prisoner chosen by myself.

Augustine's theory of original sin further enhanced the Christian notion of human depravity. He preached that sin's aftereffects were so great that they affected human reason and will as well. The tendency of humanity is toward self-love and disobedience to God, or what Augustine refers to as lust, a disordered desire that drives people away from God and toward idolatry and selfishness. Augustine argued that without God's assistance, humans are incapable of choosing good or coming back to God in this morally corrupted state. Given the depth of human need, grace is a **"radical necessity"** in the human condition.

As Augustine and several theologians after him taught, grace is necessary for salvation and not only an optional addition for moral advancement in light of our complete depravity. The only thing that can heal the rift that sin has made between the Divine and humans is God's grace. In his epistle to the Romans, the apostle Paul emphasizes the need for grace, to paraphrase **Romans 3:23-24**, for all have sinned and are falling short of the glory of God, and all are justified freely by His grace through the redemption that came by Christ Jesus. This demonstrates that salvation is wholly the consequence of God's grace and not of human deservingness or accomplishment.

The early Church Fathers stressed this fact. One of the most respected preachers of the early Church, St. John Chrysostom (349–407 AD), stated in his sermons: "When we were enemies, God was reconciled to us by the death of His Son." Grace is the ultimate gift. In addition to freeing us from our sins, He has also bestowed upon us all of His blessings and shown us how much He values us. Chrysostom emphasizes that grace is more than only sin forgiveness; it is also the manifestation of God's favor and love, which changes believers from God's enemies into his cherished children.

Grace is understood in Christian theology as an undeserved gift that God freely bestows. As **Ephesians 2:8-9** famously teaches: "For by grace you have been saved, through faith—and this is not from yourselves, it is the gift of God—not by works, so that no one can boast." These words reveal the foundational Christian belief that salvation is not a matter of human striving or merit but is entirely the result of God's loving initiative. Left to their own devices, humans could never earn God's favor or forgiveness; it is freely given and entirely gratuitous.

Beyond the theological concept of justification—that is, being made right with God—grace is also the power by which God transforms and heals the wounded human soul. The early Church understood grace not only as a legal pardon but also as a transformative force. It is divine life itself, infused into the believer, enabling them to live according to God's will. This is sometimes referred to as sanctifying grace, the grace that makes a person holy.

St. Augustine famously said, "Give what you command, and command what you will," acknowledging that even the ability to obey God's commands is a result of His grace. Humans, left in their sin, cannot live righteously without God's help. This is the work of grace within the soul—renewing the mind, healing the heart, and strengthening the will. As St. Paul writes in **Philippians 2:13**: "For it is God who works in you to will and to act in order to fulfill His good purpose."

Despite humanity's profound fallenness and incapacity to restore itself, grace reveals the tender mercy of God. It is, in a sense, scandalous—so great is its generosity and its free bestowal upon those who are utterly undeserving. The sheer magnitude of God's grace has been a source of wonder and praise throughout the history of Christianity.

As St. Bernard of Clairvaux (1090–1153 AD) eloquently wrote, "Grace is glory begun, and glory is grace consummated."

Human limitations do not bind this grace but flow from the infinite love and goodness of God. It is this divine grace, expressed most fully in the person and work of Jesus Christ, that redeems humanity from the clutches of sin and death. As **John 1:16-17** declares, "Out of His fullness we have all received grace in place of grace already given. For the law was given through Moses; grace and truth came through Jesus Christ."

Furthermore, grace is frequently seen to be a gift given freely and without demand or pressure, reflecting God's sovereign will. The nature of grace and human free will has long been a topic of discussion among theologians. While some traditions, like Calvinism, emphasize the unstoppable nature of God's grace, others, like Arminianism, contend that people have the freedom to accept or reject God's offer of grace. The fundamental idea of grace —that it is a divine effort independent of human action or deservingness—remains true, notwithstanding these theological complexities.

Grace impacts a believer's life in numerous ways. It offers fresh life and spiritual emancipation from the shackles of sin. Simply said, grace is God's love and mercy toward us in spite of the fact that we don't deserve it. This grace has a profound impact on believers' lives. It enables people to know the abiding love and forgiveness of God, regardless of their previous transgressions. This knowledge is reassuring because it demonstrates that God's love is predicated not on our goodness but rather on His own.

Despite humanity's profound fallenness and incapacity to restore itself, grace reveals the tender mercy of God. It is, in a sense, scandalous—so great is its generosity and its free bestowal upon those who are utterly undeserving. The sheer magnitude of God's grace has been a source of wonder and praise throughout the history of Christianity. As St. Bernard of Clairvaux (1090–1153 AD) eloquently wrote, "Grace is glory begun, and glory is grace consummated."

Human limitations do not bind this grace but flow from the infinite love and goodness of God. It is this divine grace, expressed most fully in the person and work of Jesus Christ, that redeems humanity from the clutches of sin and death. As **John 1:16-17** declares, "Out of His fullness we have all received grace in place of grace already given. For the law was given through Moses; grace and truth came through Jesus Christ."

God's grace also inspires people to live differently. When people genuinely comprehend and embrace God's grace, they are frequently moved to gratitude and a desire to please God. In addition to forgiving, grace transforms, fostering spiritual development and a life of kindness, tolerance, and love for others.

Simply said, grace is God's love and mercy toward us in spite of the fact that we don't deserve it. This grace has a profound impact on believers' lives. It enables people to know the abiding love and forgiveness of God, regardless of their previous transgressions. This knowledge is reassuring because it demonstrates that God's love is predicated not on our goodness but rather on His own.

God's grace also inspires people to live differently. When people genuinely comprehend and embrace God's grace, they are frequently moved to gratitude and a desire to please God. In addition to forgiving, grace transforms, fostering spiritual development and a life of kindness, tolerance, and love for others.

Grace is, therefore, both an external and internal reality. It justifies the sinner before God, and it sanctifies the soul, enabling believers to grow in holiness and virtue. This ongoing transformation is often described as a process of becoming more like Christ through the continual work of the Holy Spirit. As **Titus 2:11-12** states, "For the grace of God has appeared that offers salvation to all people. It teaches us to say 'No' to ungodliness and worldly passions and to live self-controlled, upright, and godly lives in this present age."

Grace is essential to Christianity. It demonstrates God's unwavering love and His willingness to interact with people. God's grace is always present, and it welcomes people back with open arms, regardless of how distant they may feel from Him.

CHAPTER 5
FORGIVENESS

A fundamental component of Christian theology, forgiveness is closely linked to God's grace. Fundamentally, forgiveness is letting go of resentment, hatred, or the need for retaliation against someone who has harmed or offended you. It is an act of relinquishing the weight that anger and bitterness bring, both emotionally and spiritually. Forgiveness is not only a moral virtue but also a vital component of practicing Christianity. Its foundation is found in the teachings and example of Jesus Christ, who throughout His life, death, and resurrection, personified forgiveness.

According to the Bible, forgiveness is essential to living a Christian life. Jesus, in His Sermon on the Mount, encouraged His disciples to forgive others as they hope to be forgiven by God:

"For if you forgive others their trespasses, your heavenly Father will also forgive you, but if you do not forgive others their trespasses, neither will your Father forgive your trespasses" (**Matthew 6:14-15**).

This emphasizes the idea of showing others the same kindness and grace in order to receive God's forgiveness. Thus, forgiveness becomes a means of expressing God's kindness and love in a world that is frequently characterized by injustice and strained relationships.

Forgiveness is a heavenly mandate for Christians, not just a voluntary action. Jesus' final act of pardon on the cross was expressed in His prayer, "Father, forgive them, for they know not what they do" (**Luke 23:34**) - serves as the supreme model.

Early Christian theologians and saints emphasized forgiveness's importance and power. When considering forgiveness, St. Augustine of Hippo once said, "Resentment is like drinking poison and waiting for the other person to die." Augustine cautions in this passage that the victim of unforgiveness suffers more than the wrongdoer. His message is consistent with the idea that forgiveness has a transformational power, not just for the forgiven but also for the giver.

The famous preacher St. John Chrysostom also highlighted the value of forgiveness in his works, saying that "just as a spark sets fire to everything, so does a soul inflamed with anger destroy the soul that harbors it." Chrysostom emphasizes in how a person's soul might be consumed by unforgiveness, resulting in spiritual destruction. Like many of the early Christian theologians, he believed that forgiveness was the first step toward spiritual well-being, inner peace, and contact with God.

Forgiveness is also strongly related to the grace of God, as it represents God's readiness to forgive humanity. As Paul states in **Ephesians 4:32**, Christians are obligated to extend forgiveness to others in proportion as God has extended it to them. "Be kind and compassionate to one another, forgiving each other, just as in Christ God forgave you."

This verse serves as a reminder to believers that the grace bestowed upon them ought to motivate them to bestow the same grace upon others, so establishing a merciful circle that reflects the divine relationship.

Forgiveness was frequently viewed in the early Church as a means of mending people as well as communities. According to the teachings of St. Gregory the Great, "when a man overcomes injury by forgiving his enemies, nothing is more pleasing to God." Gregory saw forgiveness as an action that promotes peace throughout the Christian society and brings one closer to God in addition to being a personal virtue.

Christian doctrine holds that forgiveness is not always simple. It frequently takes a lot of courage and humility, particularly when there has been severe hurt…and it might be the most courageous thing you will ever do. On the other hand, it is believed to be necessary for spiritual development and to be a reflection of God's forgiveness. When St. Francis of Assisi prayed, "It is in pardoning that we are pardoned," he aptly expressed this feeling. In this way, forgiveness becomes a freely given and accepted gift and grace that calms the hearts of the forgiver and the forgiven.

The capacity of Christian forgiveness to mend and rebuild damaged relationships is among its most potent features. God's desire for harmony and peace among His creation is reflected in the Bible's constant calls for Christians to be agents of reconciliation. Reconciliation is facilitated by forgiveness, which turns strained bonds into chances for development, healing, and love.

The apostle Paul wrote a great deal about how Christians should extend forgiveness to one another in the spirit of Christ. He encourages believers to "bear with each other and forgive one another if any of you has a grievance against someone" in **Colossians 3:13**. Pardon as the Lord has pardoned you. Paul highlights here that forgiveness is a collective obligation as much as a personal one.

The well-being and cohesion of the Christian community depend on it. Without forgiveness, relationships stay strained, and the Christian community cannot represent the love of Christ to the world.

The story of Joseph and his brothers is among the most captivating parables of forgiveness found in the Bible.

There are a lot of us who are familiar with this story. Inspired by jealousy, Joseph's brothers betrayed him, and he was sold into slavery. Despite his struggles, he overcame them to rise to prominence in Egypt.

His siblings came asking for assistance during a famine years later, not realizing that the strong man they were assisting was actually their own brother whom they had betrayed.

The choice Joseph makes is where the story takes a turn. Rather than taking retribution, he decided to forgive his brothers.

The story offers a potent interpersonal lesson. It demonstrates to us that forgiving someone means letting go of the resentment that keeps us stuck rather than forgetting the past.

One of the most moving tales of compassion and divine forgiveness is found in the Gospel of John (**John 8:1–11**) when Jesus pardons the adulterous woman. A woman caught in adultery was brought to Jesus by the Pharisees and professors of the law in this potent story as a test of Jesus' willingness to uphold the Law of Moses, which required that such a woman be stoned. The atmosphere was tense, with the audience poised to pass judgment. However, in His boundless wisdom, Jesus uses the circumstances to teach us about self-reflection, grace, and mercy.

Jesus knelt down and scribbled in the mud rather than condemning her before speaking His well-known words:

"Let him who is without sin among you be the first to throw a stone at her." **(John 8:7**)

The crowd considered their own transgressions after hearing him speak. They departed one by one, starting with the eldest. Next, Jesus faced the woman and uttered:

"Where are they, woman? Has nobody criticized you?

She said, "No one, Lord."

Jesus then answered, "Go and sin no more from now on; neither do I condemn you." **(John 8:10–11**)

In addition to being an act of forgiveness, this instance reveals Jesus' teaching that divine kindness wins out over legalism and condemnation. Additionally, it demonstrates His regard for the worth and dignity of every human soul, regardless of background.

Doctor of the Church St. Teresa of Avila often spoke about God's kindness as a means of transforming us, saying, "O souls! It is not about failing but about repenting and having faith in order to receive God's mercy. (Castle Interior)

Her remarks echo what Jesus said to the lady at the end: "Go, and sin no more from now on." It is a call to change, to put sin behind you and begin afresh. Absolution is only one aspect of forgiveness; another is being granted another opportunity to lead a more virtuous life.

In his pastoral writings, eminent theologian St. Gregory the Great discussed the restorative power of forgiveness, stating that "nothing is more pleasing to God than when a man overcomes injury by forgiving his enemies." St. Gregory understood that forgiveness not only mends broken bonds but also draws the forgiver nearer to God. By forgiving others, Christians grow spiritually and become more like God. They also emulate God's own forgiveness.

Healing occurs on a personal level when forgiveness is given. Christians can achieve peace and wholeness by letting go of their anger and resentment. Forgiveness frees people from the emotional burden of past wrongs and alters the heart, enabling them to move on from their previous wrongdoings. The believer experiences both emotional and spiritual healing as a result of this healing, which makes room for God's grace to enter their lives more readily.

It would not be incorrect to assume that the idea of forgiveness is vital in Christianity, especially when they are in need of it. However, as discussed, it can also be quite difficult to forgive others, particularly when we believe we have been mistreated severely. However, a life lived in freedom and a connection with God are inextricably linked to forgiveness.

However, it might not be as easy and straightforward as it sounds. Some people believe that they have made so many mistakes in life—or that others have made mistakes upon them—that they cannot possibly believe that God will ever pardon them and grant them a fresh start. However, according to the Bible, the only sin that God is unable to pardon is the evil that we refuse to acknowledge. David, the greatest king of Israel, committed many terrible sins, such as adultery and murderous plots. Still, he was able to win God's pardon by saying, "I have sinned against the LORD" (**2 Samuel 12:13**). God is a forgiving God, and he can and will pardon everything we have done, said, or thought. Provided that we ask him.

You also need to look at Jesus Christ, the ultimate forgiver. Our shepherd is the ideal example of forgiveness at the core of Christian theology. His life and teachings reveal

God's great and unwavering compassion for people, and His crucifixion is the most profound act of forgiveness recorded in the Bible. Jesus' capacity for forgiveness demonstrates the extent of God's love and compassion, even in the face of great injustice and suffering.

Jesus's crucifixion is one of the most moving episodes of His life. Jesus prayed for forgiveness while hanging on the cross, knowing that He was being crucified by the very people He came to save: "Father, forgive them, for they do not know what they are doing" (**Luke 23:34**). Speaking in the middle of His suffering, this act of forgiveness shows the character of God, who is quick to pardon even serious transgressions.

In addition to serving as an illustration of God's pardon, Jesus' prayer on the cross serves as a role model for Christians. It demonstrates that even in the most trying and unbearable circumstances, forgiveness is possible. It also serves as a reminder to believers that the character of the one who extends forgiveness matters more than the deservingness of the offender. Jesus pardoned His executioners because His compassion for them outweighed their transgressions, not because they deserved it. Likewise, Christians are expected to extend forgiveness—not because the one who harmed them merits it, but rather because Christ extended it to them first.

In his own last moments, St. Stephen, the first Christian martyr, imitated this example set by Christ. Stephen pleaded, "Lord, do not hold this sin against them." At the same time, he was being stoned (**Acts 7:60**). Like Jesus, Stephen forgave his persecutors, exhibiting the transformative power of forgiveness in the life of a believer. In addition to reflecting Christ's teachings, this act of forgiveness in the face of violence encourages Christians to practice their religion with the same bravery and grace.

Therefore, experiencing divine grace is the cornerstone of having a forgiving spirit. We are rescued only because of grace. We exist only because of grace. We have received forgiveness via grace. Consequently, the purpose of forgiveness is to express our thankfulness for the kindness bestowed upon us. Once more, Jesus' story highlights a person who refused to behave in a way that reflected and matched God's goodness and instead took the favor he was given for granted. Why is forgiveness necessary? Merely because God is merciful to us. It is important to emphasize that the God of grace orders us to exercise grace in response to that charge.

The forgiveness found in the Bible is quite beautiful. Our guilt is removed when we have a trusting faith in Jesus' sacrifice and fully submit to God and His plan. The blood of Jesus Christ pays the entire cost of our sins. God's forgiveness absolves us of our transgressions and pains.

According to **Hebrews 8:12**, "And their iniquities will I remember no more," He clears the slate and forgets our transgressions. When God pardons our sins, and we pardon one another, what amazing freedom we can feel. This is something that your life and heart can also experience. Come now unto the Lord!

CHAPTER 6

FIRST HEALING

"Christ Himself came as a physician to heal the sickness of the soul, for He alone has the medicine of salvation," penned St. Augustine of Hippo, highlighting the close relationship between God's healing mercy and His divine ability. In Christianity, healing is a holistic process that takes into account a person's spiritual, emotional, and interpersonal well-being in addition to simply restoring their physical health. Believers receive healing because of God's love and grace, which is not just for bodily illnesses. It includes the mending of hearts torn by sin, sorrow, and estrangement from God as well as the healing of the soul and repair of strained relationships.

The Gospels portray Jesus as the Great Healer, a supernatural doctor whose touch could heal the soul in addition to the body. His healing miracles, which include recovering lepers and giving blind people their sight, are like sunlight penetrating a storm cloud and bringing hope where there was only despair. Like a seed buried deep in the dirt that grows into a flourishing tree, every act of healing is a window into God's infinite mercy, an external expression of His internal grace.

In addition to demonstrating His omnipotence, Christ's healing mission was a powerful act of empathy as He understood the depth of human sorrow in the same way a mother understands her child's anguish. His miracles revitalized the body, mind, and soul by bringing life where there was only death, much like fresh water poured into dry soil. These healing deeds were more than just momentary consolation; they were indications that the barren, shattered earth of human existence was giving way to a verdant, lush garden of rebirth.

Jesus filled the chasm between the fragmented state of this world and the entirety of God's kingdom by His touch. His healing ministry served as evidence that God's kingdom had actually arrived on earth, bringing with it the hope of rebirth and restoration for everyone who sought it, much like the first spring blossoms heralding the end of winter. Every miracle served as a preview of the ultimate restoration that was yet to occur: a world devoid of illness, grief, and death, in which everything would be renewed.

Christ's healing miracles were planned acts of kindness that were motivated by God's love for His creation rather than haphazard demonstrations of His power. Every miracle reveals a greater truth: that God's grace, through Christ, goes into the deepest recesses of human sorrow to provide both instant comfort and unending hope.

This chapter will examine the Christian understanding of healing, how it relates to God's grace, and how it expresses God's compassion and love for those in need. Healing, whether it takes the shape of a spiritual or physical restoration, is evidence of the transforming power of God's grace made known through Jesus Christ.

The atoning work that Christ completed on the cross is at the center of this redemptive healing. **Isaiah 53:5** prophetically declares, "But he was pierced for our transgressions, he was crushed for our iniquities; the punishment that brought us peace was on him, and by his wounds we are healed." This verse, which is frequently quoted in Christian theology, demonstrates that Christ's suffering serves as both the means of healing and a substitute for humanity's sins. Christians believe that God restores both physical and spiritual health through His wounds. Because healing is a direct outcome of Jesus's sacrifice, it is directly associated with His redeeming work.

The promise of total recovery and rejuvenation is further supported by Christ's resurrection. "He himself bore our sins in his body on the cross, so that we might die to sins and live for righteousness; by his wounds, you have been healed," the apostle Peter writes in **1 Peter 2:24**, reflecting on Christ's work. This healing offers deliverance from the grip of sin and the prospect of eternal life, reaching not only the physical body but also the fundamental heart of human existence.

According to Christian doctrine, the healing that Christ offers beyond this life. While God may heal physical ailments, believers are most assured of receiving eternal life and the promise of resurrection in a new creation devoid of death, pain, and suffering. The Bible offers a glimpse of this promise for the future in **Revelation 21:4**: "He will wipe every tear from their eyes." Because the old order of things has vanished, there won't be any more deaths, grief, sobs, or agony. This verse depicts the full realization of healing and the permanent mending of the world's brokenness as the pinnacle of God's redemptive mission.

"Because the Son of God became man so that we might become God; He manifested Himself by a body so that we might receive the idea of the unseen Father; and He endured the insolence of men so that we might inherit immortality," wrote St. Athanasius of Alexandria, one of the early Christian theologians, in a beautiful description of this final restoration. Athanasius discusses here the last change brought about by Christ, namely immortality and one with God. This healing from God is more than physical well-being; it provides an everlasting repair of the body and soul.

Throughout His earthly mission, Jesus performed healing miracles that were both compassionate deeds and prophetic of the coming of God's kingdom. All of Christ's healing acts, including raising the dead, helping the lame walk, and opening the eyes of the blind, were a preview of the complete healing that God has promised to His people. Jesus said, "Go back and report to John what you hear and see: The blind receive sight, the lame walk, those who have leprosy are cleansed, the deaf hear, the dead are raised, and the good news is proclaimed to the poor," in response to John the Baptist's disciples asking Him if He was the Messiah (**Matthew 11:4-5**). These wonders served as a taste of God's reign.

According to Christian doctrine, God's redemptive mission for humanity includes healing in a very significant way. God's original plan included not only the physical and spiritual welfare of His people but also the salvation and restoration of the entire world. All who believe are offered the ultimate healing through the death and resurrection of Jesus Christ. This promise speaks to the complete restoration of humanity's broken condition and goes beyond the momentary relief of physical ailments. It includes freedom from sin, eternal life, and the hope of a new creation.

Christianity places a strong emphasis on the idea that God can heal a person's body, soul, and spirit in addition to mending their physical illnesses. "To save, to heal, to make whole" is another meaning of the Greek word *sozo*, which means "salvation." The Christian view that physical suffering and deterioration were brought about by humanity's fall into sin is reflected in this holistic approach to healing. As the Savior, Jesus came to repair the harm done by sin and bring people back to the state of wholeness that God intended.

In **Luke 17:19**, after curing 10 lepers, Jesus tells the one who came back to thank Him, "Rise and go; your faith has made you well." "Made you well" suggests a more profound, spiritual cure than just physically curing leprosy. Therefore, Jesus' healings were not merely one-off miracles; rather, they were essential to His goal of giving humanity back its wholeness.

One of the most significant early Church Fathers, St. Basil the Great, eloquently explained the relationship between body, soul, and spirit, comparing it to the interdependence of life itself. He emphasized that just as a vine cannot grow fruit without its roots, so too the soul cannot flourish without being sustained by the Spirit of God. "The body does not continue to live when it is deprived of the soul, nor does the soul subsist apart from the Spirit of God," he wrote. This striking artwork emphasizes how God's presence is the wellspring of all life, spiritual and physical.

According to this perspective, a human being is a complexly interwoven whole rather than just a collection of discrete components. The spirit is the fuel that keeps the flame of the soul burning brightly inside the body, which is like a delicate vessel. Without God, the body becomes lifeless as the soul fades and flickers. This metaphor highlights the deeper reality that while physical health is brief, only Christ can provide true healing—the type that restores a person's body as well as their very nature.

Basil's redemption vision alludes to an everlasting and interior divine healing. He argues that the ultimate goal of the Christian life is the unification of the soul with God via Christ, whereby one is changed into completeness and immortality rather than just being healed of physical disorders. It's like a broken vessel being fixed by master potter, who not only fixes the flaws but also gives it enduring beauty and strength instead of human hands.

This all-encompassing healing restores something fundamental to human beings, surpassing the momentary alleviation of sorrow. It seems like a life-giving rush of water turns an arid desert into a blooming garden. Similar to this, the soul, which was before lifeless and cut off from God, is given new life and nourishment by Christ's love and transformed into a dynamic, living image of the divine.

Basil perfectly captures the Christian view that the soul's oneness with God is the source of true healing rather than earthly cures. This connection is like a wandering star returning to its proper location in the sky, where it shines brilliantly in the light of the Creator. The ultimate healing —where body, soul, and spirit are made whole in the eternal life God promises—can only be experienced in this divine relationship—through Christ. This bridge unites humanity and the divine.

Regarding the Church's role in healing, St. Cyril of Jerusalem remarked, "The Spirit comes gently and makes himself known by his fragrance." He is the one who gives out gifts of kindness and cures the wounded; He is light and healing. With the help of the Holy Spirit, the Church serves as a vehicle for God's healing presence in the world, offering people in need of both spiritual and physical healing as well as reconciliation.

In summary, Christianity argues that healing is a component of God's larger redemptive purpose for humanity rather than an isolated occurrence. Believers are provided the ultimate healing via the death and resurrection of Christ: eternal life, liberation from sin, and the prospect of a new creation devoid of death and suffering. The accounts of Jesus' miracles in the Gospels guide Christians toward the day when God will completely mend everything that is broken and serve as a taste of this eternal restoration.

CHAPTER 7

THE POWER OF FAITH AND PRAYER

Faith and prayer are two powerful pillars in the Christian journey, deeply interwoven with the believer's experience of divine healing and restoration. In the New Testament, faith is often portrayed as the key that unlocks God's power, and prayer is the channel through which that power flows. Both are more than religious duties—they are intimate conversations with God, expressions of trust in His will, and acts of surrender to His wisdom.

At its core, faith is more than intellectual belief in God's existence; it is an active trust in His character, promises, and ability to intervene in the lives of His people. Hebrews 11:1 defines faith as "the assurance of things hoped for, the conviction of things not seen." This assurance is what carries believers through the trials of life, giving them confidence that God's unseen hand is at work in every situation.

In the Gospels, Jesus repeatedly emphasizes the importance of faith in the context of healing. For instance, in Mark 5:34, after healing a woman who had been suffering from a hemorrhage for twelve years, Jesus tells her, "Daughter, your faith has healed you. Go in peace and be freed from your suffering." This passage highlights the relationship between faith and divine healing—her belief in Jesus' power and her boldness to approach Him in faith brought about her physical and spiritual restoration.

Faith, however, is not blind optimism. It is a profound reliance on God, trusting that He knows best, even when His answers to prayer differ from our expectations. The Bible is full of stories where faith in God's ultimate goodness sustained individuals through times of great suffering, when immediate healing was not granted. Job, for example, endured incredible pain and loss, yet his faith remained intact. His declaration, "Though He slay me, yet will I trust in Him" (Job 13:15), is a testament to the depth of faith that transcends circumstances.

While faith activates the healing power of God, prayer is the means by which believers communicate their desires, struggles, and hopes to Him. The Bible repeatedly affirms the importance of persistent, fervent prayer. James 5:16 declares, "The prayer of a righteous person is powerful and effective." This simple statement encapsulates the Christian belief that prayer, when offered with faith and humility, can move mountains. Through prayer, believers partner with God in His work of healing and restoration.

Prayer, like faith, involves both submission and action. In his letters, the apostle Paul emphasizes the role of prayer in the life of the believer. In Philippians 4:6-7, he urges, "Do not be anxious about anything, but in every situation, by prayer and petition, with thanksgiving, present your requests to God. And the peace of God, which transcends all understanding, will guard your hearts and your minds in Christ Jesus." Here, Paul ties the act of prayer to inner peace and emotional healing. In this way, prayer becomes more than a way of asking for specific outcomes; it is a means of drawing nearer to God and receiving His peace amid life's challenges.

In the Gospels, we see Jesus frequently retreating to pray, often before key moments in His ministry. These times of prayer were moments of deep communion with the Father, where Jesus sought strength and guidance. His prayer in the Garden of Gethsemane, just before His arrest, is one of the most poignant moments in the New Testament. "Father, if you are willing, take this cup from me; yet not my will, but yours be done" (Luke 22:42). This prayer exemplifies ultimate submission to God's will, even when faced with suffering. In Christian teaching, Jesus is the model of perfect prayer—He teaches believers to seek God's will above their own, even when it leads through the valley of suffering.

In addition to Jesus' own prayers, the Gospels record numerous instances where He teaches others to pray and highlights the power of prayer in healing. One of the most well-known is the story of the Roman centurion in Matthew 8:5-13, whose faith in Jesus' authority is so strong that he believes a mere word from Jesus will heal his servant. Jesus marvels at the centurion's faith and says, "Truly I tell you, I have not found anyone in Israel with such great faith." The centurion's prayer of faith, though brief and humble, demonstrates the profound connection between belief in God's power and the act of prayer.

The Christian tradition teaches that prayer and faith are not merely personal spiritual practices but are also communal. In the book of Acts, the early Church often gathered together in prayer, seeking God's guidance, protection, and healing as a body of believers. One notable example is when Peter is imprisoned, and the Church prays fervently for his release. In response, an angel of the Lord frees Peter from his chains and leads him out of the prison (Acts 12:5-11). This story serves as a powerful reminder that the prayers of God's people, when united in faith, can lead to miraculous outcomes.

However, the mystery of faith and prayer is that they do not always result in immediate healing or deliverance. There are times when God's will includes a journey through suffering rather than instant relief from it. The apostle Paul himself experienced this when he prayed three times for God to remove a "thorn in the flesh," a mysterious affliction that caused him great distress. Instead of removing the thorn, God responded, "My grace is sufficient for you, for my power is made perfect in weakness" (2 Corinthians 12:9). This passage illustrates a profound truth in Christian teaching: that God's power is often revealed most fully in times of human weakness and vulnerability.

While physical healing is a significant aspect of Christian faith, the deeper healing of the soul—freedom from sin and the promise of eternal life—is the ultimate goal of God's redemptive work. Jesus' resurrection, the cornerstone of the Christian faith, is the greatest act of divine healing, conquering death itself. Through His death and resurrection, believers are assured that even if they do not experience physical healing in this life, they will be fully restored in the life to come. The apostle John's vision in Revelation 21:4 points to this future reality: "He will wipe every tear from their eyes. There will be no more death or mourning or crying or pain, for the old order of things has passed away."

Faith and prayer are, therefore, more than just tools for temporary relief; they are pathways to a deeper relationship with God, where trust in His sovereign will and acceptance of His plan lead to ultimate healing. The Christian life is marked by a balance between asking for God's intervention in the here and now and trusting in His promise of future restoration.

In this chapter, we have explored the centrality of faith and prayer in the Christian experience of healing. Whether through miraculous recovery or the strength to endure suffering, these two spiritual practices bind believers to God's heart, assuring them of His presence and His power. They are the means through which God's grace flows into the brokenness of this world, bringing hope, comfort, and the promise of ultimate restoration.